sound parade my sound parade
sound parade my sound parade
sound parade my sound parade
sound parade my sound parade
sound parade my sound parade
sound parade my sound parade
sound parade my sound parade
sound parade my sound parade
sound parade my sound parade
sound parade my sound parade
sound parade my sound parade
sound parade my sound parade
sound parade my sound parade

my sound parade my sound para
my sound parade my sound para
my sound parade my sound para
my sound parade my sound para
my sound parade my sound para
my sound parade my sound para
my sound parade my sound para
my sound parade my sound para
my sound parade my sound para
my sound parade my sound para
my sound parade my sound para
my sound parade my sound par

My Sound Parade

Library of Congress Cataloging-in-Publication Data
Moncure, Jane Belk.
My sound parade / by Jane Belk Moncure.
p. cm.
Summary: A parade of characters and animals
introduces the letters of the alphabet.
ISBN 1-56766-766-X (lib. bdg. : alk. paper)
[1. Alphabet. 2. Animals–Fiction.
3. Parades–Fiction. 4. Stories in rhyme.] I. Title.
PZ8.3.M72 My   2000
[E]—dc21   99-055405

My Sound Parade

Jane Belk Moncure

illustrated by Colin King

The Child's World

Clap your hands. Tap your feet.
A parade is coming down the street.

Little a and an alligator
lead the way.

"You can come along, too," they say.

Here comes Little  with a baby baboon,

and a bear on a bicycle with a balloon.

Little

rides a camel with a cat and a clown.

Little d and some ducks dance up and down.

Little rides an
elephant.
Some elves
are in a box.

Here comes Little

with five frogs and a fox.

Little

plays a guitar
and sings a song.
Some goats and a gorilla dance along.

Little
blows
his horn,

and a hippo hops
upside down until he stops.

Little skips along

with her insect zoo.

Little and Jumbo skip along, too.

Here comes

Little

and a kangaroo.

Little

will take you for a ride
with a lamb and a lion. Step inside!

Little

comes by with a moose
and some mice. And three
little monkeys. They are very nice.

Little  has nickels for everyone.

Little

and an ostrich
join in the fun.

Little

rides her pony with piglets three.

Little **q** calls quietly,

"Please wait for me."

Little

has a reindeer.

You can ride it, too . . . with a rabbit, and
a rooster singing "Cock-a-doodle-doo."

Little and a sailor skip along with six silly seals singing a song.

Little

drives a truck with a box full of toys.

Little u

has umbrellas for all the girls and boys.

Little has lots of valentines
that say, "We like you."

Little and her whale say,
"We like you, too."

Where are they going? Do not ask me.

Ask Little  and . . .

and

They may tell you they are
going to the animal zoo.

To the brand new Sound Box animal zoo.

insects

camel

Jumbo

alligator

frog

elephant

hippo

lion

gorilla

fro

ostrich

frog

baboon

dog

nightingales

umbrella bird

reindeer

whale

seals

rhino

zebra

pony

moose

yak

kitten

tiger

kitten

You can come, too!

ABOUT THE AUTHOR AND ILLUSTRATOR

Jane Belk Moncure began her writing career when she was in kindergarten. She has never stopped writing. Many of her children's stories and poems have been published, to the delight of young readers, including her son Jim, whose childhood experiences found their way into many of her books.

Mrs. Moncure's writing is based upon an active career in early childhood education.
A recipient of an M.A. degree from Columbia University, Mrs. Moncure has taught and directed nursery, kindergarten, and primary grade programs in California, New York, Virginia, and North Carolina. As a former member of the faculties of Virginia Commonwealth University and the University of Richmond, she taught prospective teachers in early childhood education.

Mrs. Moncure has travelled extensively abroad, studying early childhood programs in the United Kingdom, The Netherlands, and Switzerland. She was the first president of the Virginia Association for Early Childhood Education and received its award for outstanding service to young children.

A resident of North Carolina, Mrs. Moncure is currently a full-time writer and educational consultant. She is married to Dr. James A. Moncure, former vice president of Elon College.

Colin King studied at the Royal College of Art, London. He started his freelance career as an illustrator, working for magazines and advertising agencies.

He began drawing pictures for children's books in 1976 and has illustrated over sixty titles to date.

Included in a wide variety of subjects are a best-selling children's encyclopedia and books about spies and detectives.

His books have been translated into several languages, including Japanese and Hebrew. He has four grown-up children and lives in Suffolk, England, with his wife, three dogs, and a cat.